HENRY FICKLE
AND THE MAGIC DRAGON
OF PENNSYLVANIA

BY
MICHELE MACK

COVER ART BY JAMES BROWNE

COVER DESIGN AND INTERIOR DESIGN BY NATHAN BILLMAN

THE SORCERER'S PRESS

FOR PENNSYLVANIA FANS

ISBN: 978-0-9667747-4-0

10 9 8 7 6 5 4 3 2 1

Printed in the U.S.A.

First edition, 2010

Cover art by James Browne

Cover design and interior design by Nathan Billman

Every once in a while a book comes along that uplifts the minds of kids and adults alike. This delightful story is simple reading, but its impact is monumental. My intent is to inspire you to believe in the impossible!

CHAPTER ONE

Not for the first time, an unexpected explosion had erupted over the hill of Windy Drive. The neighbors had been woken in the early hours of the morning by a loud blast from the Fickle estate.

"Second time this week!" Mr. Collingsworth roared to his wife, who was now sitting bolt upright. "That boy is a nuisance! I'll be having another talk with his uncle!"

Meanwhile, back at home, young Henry tried, yet again, to explain.

"S-Sorry," he muttered. "I must have mixed the wrong ingredients. If I could just find the right mixture—"

Uncle Berk, a portly little man in a wrinkly, old suit, looked on the contrary, quite calm.

"No need to fret," said Uncle Berk in a reassuring tone, surveying his only nephew. "Carry on, Henry. You're going to be a famous inventor someday, you'll see." He glanced out the study window, while puffing on a fat cigar, a cloud of smoke billowing in the air.

"Er ... Sir?" blurted Henry.

But Uncle Berk seemed to be in quiet contemplation.

The young inventor's heart lightened considerably, as he raced out of the room. Henry Fickle was a very intuitive boy—a boy that would later prove to be *very* important someday. And if the town folk were not approving of his odd-almost-obsessive behavior—well, it didn't matter. Uncle Berk was a kind-hearted, patient man who had always given his nodding approval.

At times, Henry felt alone and disconnected from the rest of the world. He missed his parents, his friends (though they never seemed to last too long), and especially, family vacations.

Most unfortunately, Henry's dear mother died when he was

born. Later, his father remarried and he was raised by his wicked stepmother. She randomly created rules, making living unbearable.

After his father's untimely death, he inherited the Fickle estate and half his money. His stepmother had gotten the other half. Soon after, she left town with a hefty pocketbook. He never heard from her again.

Since then, his father's only brother, Berk had been raising the boy, because Henry Fickle wasn't a normal boy. As a matter of fact, he was as strange as could be.

After school, and into the wee hours of the morning, he'd spend endless hours in the garage, tinkering with odd inventions. But the noise and unexpected explosions caused folks to talk. He was known as the weird kid, teased by his classmates. Teachers kept him after school for freeing caged mice from Science classrooms, and the town council was concerned that his erratic behavior would reach city newspapers. Clearly, the small town of Willow Creek did not need that kind of publicity.

Henry lived like a hermit, lonely and confused. He had no trustworthy friends, except Uncle Berk. He was convinced he'd lost his mind. He just wanted to be normal like other kids ...

But it never happened.

So Henry had been brought up by his dead father's brother. An agreement had been made until the boy finished high school. He had spent most of his younger years with Uncle Berk, never understanding why street lamps along Windy Drive would pop and flicker into darkness, or why another night of experiments would black out the entire town for days, believing the town folk might be right after all.

And then, one windy night, while catching a few words of the evening news on a Zenith console radio, the young inventor's life took an unexpected turn.

CHAPTER TWO

"And halts in industrial production and construction and a severe decline in stock prices, has Americans in a state of panic. Job loses are occurring in alarming rates in the mining and logging areas." The broadcaster took a moment to clear his throat. "And now, stay tuned for a melody of music."

Henry sat frozen in his leather armchair, as he listened intently to the disturbing broadcast. What was happening? Banks and Businesses failing? Farmers in foreclosure? Millions of people jobless and homeless? And people, people losing hope ...

It was the early 1930s and the world was in the deepest, economic depression of the 20th century. Families in America feared the future, as they foraged in dumps and garbage cans looking for food.

Since money was scarce, people used entertainment to escape the hardships. Movies, parlor and board games were popular. Radio gave Americans a chance to share a common experience. People gathered around, tuning in to the hottest boxing matches and baseball games, while the younger generation danced to big bands. Some even read inspirational books to make their lives happy.

Henry had no idea what was happening in the world, because he'd been preoccupied with school and his personal projects.

Years earlier, after hearing his father and stepmother arguing over political issues, he made it his business to never fill his mind with the affairs of the world. He'd leave it to others to fight over ...

But this was different. This felt personal. He lived here too. Henry's heart sank. He thought of other kids. He desperately wanted to help, but reality hit him. Clearly, he was only one person. What could *he* possibly do to help? Maybe he was being foolish, he thought. After all, he was just a kid!

Uncle Berk entered the living room carrying two cups of tea and a plate of English biscuits. He had to say something. He cleared his throat nervously.

"Er—Uncle Berk—you haven't heard the news lately, have you?" He reached forward and snatched a few of the sweet treats.

As he had expected, Uncle Berk wasn't surprised. After all, he never missed the news. In fact, every morning, as he ate a hearty breakfast, he'd tune in to the latest broadcast. Every now and then he mumbled words like "Another price increase … gasoline going through the roof," and "might as well ride a bike …"

"Yes," he said curiously. "Why?"

"I don't get it," Henry mumbled in an irritating tone. "What's going on? I mean, why are people losing their jobs and their homes? I thought America was rich!"

Uncle Berk sipped his tea, while sitting back in a matching leather armchair. Henry wondered whether he was going to address his troubled mind.

After what seemed a long while, Uncle Berk reached forward and switched off the radio. Then he leaned back and spoke a few words.

"Yes, yes, times are tough," he said sadly, shaking his head. "Many folks are discouraged—but we mustn't grumble. It does us no good." He stuffed a piece of biscuit into his wide mouth, enjoying every bite.

Henry slowly nodded.

Uncle Berk peered at Henry like he was anticipating more of his questions.

But Henry was still thinking. How could *he* change things? Clearly, he couldn't possibly solve everyone's financial issues, but he could try to lift their spirits. But how? It would take a miracle, he thought, feeling helpless.

Henry finally looked at Uncle Berk and blurted out the rest of the questions that surfaced in his mouth. "What about our Science or great inventions? What about all the smart people living in America? Can't *somebody* do something?"

After taking another sip of tea, Uncle Berk continued. "America has experienced hard times, but prosperity has always returned and will again, Henry. Each time, she becomes a stronger nation. It's just a matter of time." He peered deep into Henry's eyes. "Every generation experiences these hardships, you see, but it's what we learn from them that counts."

Henry listened with rapt attention. Uncle Berk's encouraging words were like food to his spirit. He couldn't foresee that at this very moment, his clever uncle was planting a seed in his young mind. He was being prepared for an extraordinary future. If he were told prematurely what was to come—well, the responsibility would have overwhelmed him.

"May I ask another question?" said Henry.

"Fire away, my boy."

"I've been thinking … Uncle Berk—I can't explain it—not even to myself, but I *have* to do something, I mean, I want to help other kids. Do you have any ideas?"

"Ah, the question I've been waiting for," Uncle Berk sighed, "I'm afraid I cannot tell you. This you must search for on your own … when you are ready, Henry, you will know what to do."

Henry sat there, lost for words. This was not what he expected. He was hoping for a better answer. Uncle Berk hummed a little and stared around the quiet room, which gave Henry time to dry his eyes on his shirt. When he had found his voice again, Henry said, "I'll think I'll go to the garage for a while. I'm working on something. It's not ready, yet—but it's going to be really cool." Henry's eyes were suddenly gleaming with crazed enthusiasm.

Uncle Berk looked delighted.

"Don't stay up late, Henry," he said thoughtfully. "You have school tomorrow."

After hearing those last, undesirable words, Henry's stomach dropped unpleasantly.

"Uncle Berk," said Henry suddenly, peering over his shoulder. "Er—thanks."

Uncle Berk smiled widely. Then he popped another biscuit into his mouth.

Henry walked briskly toward the door when the setting sun caught his attention.

It was a spectacular sight! He stood against the glass, staring absent-mindedly at the orange and reddish hues. Something big and dark flashed past the window, rattling the glass. He stumbled backward at once, a look of panic on his face. But when he peered again, it was gone.

"What the—?"

The room suddenly went quiet. Henry's stomach lurched. What was happening?

He turned to say something, but his uncle was already snoring. Just as well, he didn't want people thinking he was seeing things. After all, who would believe him? Nobody ever did. He dismissed the strange incident and then bolted out the door.

Henry was determined to put the disturbing news out of his head. After all, there was nothing he could do about it. Instead, he focused on his latest project, which was much more fun.

"It's my best invention ever," he had told his uncle.

Henry stood in the dusty garage, while leafing through his soiled notes. He mumbled to himself as he mixed different ingredients together. He hoped that another explosion wouldn't happen that night. If it did, he was certain Mr. Collingsworth would be calling his uncle, again.

Although he was engrossed in his work, the broadcaster's words kept surfacing in his head. For some strange reason, his brain wouldn't allow him to forget.

What can I do to help?

Henry felt exhausted. It was midnight when at last, the ambitious ten-year-old slumped over the workbench, and fell into an uneasy sleep, and that's where our story starts.

Henry dreamed that he was working on his latest invention. The only sound he heard were bubbles coming from the laboratory beakers.

How can I inspire other kids?

Henry shook his head, trying to erase America's problems, but it was a dream. He'd no sense of control, as the movie continued to unravel in his sleep state.

He carefully weighed dried nettles, grinded wolf fangs, and stewed eyes of toads. A puff of green smoke and a shrill hissing filled the garage.

Henry had a sudden idea.

He grabbed a few strands of foxtail and a pickled pig snout and dropped it into the mixture. As he mixed the strange ingredients, a low, rumbling noise reached his ears. Glass bottles tumbled to the dirt floor, shattering into pieces; the ground shook, and the work light swung uncontrollably overhead.

"Go away," Henry muttered as the pounding got louder in his head. "Not now … stop it … I'm trying to sleep …"

He opened his eyes. The noise ceased at once and was replaced by an eerie silence. Moonlight was filtering through a crack in the wide doors. For a moment, he thought Uncle Berk had woken him.

And then he saw it.

Someone was staring through the crack at him: a large, brilliant-blue, catlike eye.

Bahamut, the Platinum Dragon, Lord of the North Wind was outside the garage doors.

CHAPTER THREE

"AAAAAAAAAAARGH!"

Henry felt the blood drain out of his face, as he let out an ear-splitting scream. He stumbled backward at once, a look of panic on his face.

The mighty dragon lifted his head and peered right at Henry, a gob of saliva dribbled down his razor-sharp teeth. Then came a deafening roar.

Henry cupped his hands over his ears, trying to muffle the sound, but it was no use. The creature thrashed his spiked tail, leaving gouge marks in the earth. Torrents of fire were shooting sixty feet above into the moonlit sky from his open, fanged mouth.

The garage floor rumbled as Henry gripped the workbench. His heart was thumping wildly. He was sure Uncle Berk could hear it. The noise itself encompassed the entire estate. Henry frowned. Any moment, Mr. Collingsworth would be calling his uncle.

For a few horrible seconds, he wasn't sure whether to run or give in to the fierce dragon. He cowered against the wall, realizing he'd lost his voice. He craned his head around the hazy room and gulped. There was no escape. He wondered. What was a dragon doing *here?*

Once Henry got over the initial shock of seeing something so ancient, he started to appreciate his majestic appearance.

Towering above the garage roof, was the most mystical creature Henry had ever seen. A brilliant divine radiance surrounded the dragon, who was covered in silver-white scales like perfect mirrors. The catlike eyes were stark blue, varying in hue from icy-cold indigo to the deep cerulean glow of the sky. And his body, which glowed in the dim light, was frosty indigo.

Then, without warning, the creature stretched his spiked neck to his fullest extent toward Henry, thrusting the doors wide open. His nostrils were still smoking. His penetrating eyes lingered for a moment on Henry, as if contemplating his loyalty.

"Hummmmm," said a deep voice somewhere in the room.

Henry gasped.

He craned his head around the room, but realized he was alone.

Did the dragon say something?

"Aaaahhhh ..." the floating voice said in a pleased tone.

"Are ... are you talking to me?" faltered Henry, as his heart pounded against his chest.

But the dragon remained silent.

Then, the dragon's body suddenly turned green, as if affected by his mood. Henry prayed in silence, hoping the color green meant he was cheerful.

Henry blinked and stared at the dragon. The dragon stared back. Henry gave himself a little shake and put the silly thought out of his mind. What could he have been thinking of? It must have been his wild imagination ... yes, that would be it.

Mesmerized, Henry looked up, and saw the vertical pupils narrowing.

A hush fell over the room.

But then, to Henry's great surprise, the dragon withdrew his long neck, and suddenly bent his front knees and sank into what was an unmistakable bow.

Henry's eyes jerked open.

The hairs tickled the back of Henry's neck when the pair of catlike eyes blinked at him.

"Huh?"

When he looked again, the dragon's deep azure eyes remained still as a statue. Although the beast was ghastly looking, Henry felt a calm sense of protection. He knew, somehow, the massive creature felt him worthy.

Henry bowed his head slightly, while keeping one eye on the dragon. The dragon's eyes blinked, again.

"What the—?"

This time, Henry took a tentative step forward. He moved, somewhat reluctantly toward the powerful creature.

To his surprise, the dragon dropped his scaly head to the ground.

Henry's mouth fell open as the full impact of what he was seeing hit him. He reached out and patted his head. The dragon, once again, blinked.

Henry smiled.

He didn't know why, but he felt an instant connection, as if he were meeting an old friend. The dragon's eyes grew brighter and brighter.

Moments later, he sensed something happening, as if the creature wanted to say something. *But how was that possible?*

At last, a deep voice echoed from the dragon's body. It was so pronounced that it appeared to be from nowhere in particular, but rather emanated everywhere.

"Greetings!" spoke the dragon gently-but-powerfully. "We meet at last, Henry!"

Henry drew a great shuddering breath of excitement and said, "Y-You can speak? I knew it!" Henry looked up, amazed. "H-How did you know my name?" His eyes were fixed unblinkingly on the mystical creature.

The dragon's mouth crinkled, as though the creature knew something he didn't.

A calmness stilled the evening air. Henry didn't know what to expect next, but there was no doubt something magical was happening.

CHAPTER FOUR

"You have an important mission," said the dragon in a serious tone, penetrating Henry's eyes, "but you have a choice to accept my offer or not. I've been assigned to help."

Henry thought whatever was meant about a *mission* seemed to be important. A sudden idea popped into his head. Could it be that the dragon had flown past the living room window earlier this evening? Come to think of it, he did see something flash past the glass. Had the dragon *heard* his concerns? Henry started to speak, but the dragon continued talking.

"Yes, today, you are surely needed in America, Henry, but your services are needed more in America's future! The Great Depression of the 1930s will soon be coming to an abrupt end, but in the twenty-first century, the land of opportunity will experience a great recession! This will occur in the year 2008—"

Henry's eyes bulged out. Then the horrific news traveled to his gut. *Another Great Depression?* Seconds later, his stomach dropped unpleasantly.

Before Henry had a chance to open his mouth, the dragon continued. "Your mission, Henry, will be to stop this reoccurring cycle—end its crippling consciousness from occurring in future generations. The time has come when people will finally learn, moving gracefully into a new awareness. A new America will soon dawn on the horizon."

The two stared deeply at each other for several minutes, until the dragon said a few final words.

"Yes, I will be with you, but it will be up to you to open people's hearts." The dragon shook his head. "Unfortunately, most adults still won't be ready to hear your words, but the children will listen. Let me see …" the dragon said slowly, as if to himself. "We have much to do. Yes, many children to reach …"

The stunned 10-year-old boy listened, not knowing how to file this new information, not knowing what to think, or what to say. The monumental task—the one that awaited him, had finally sunk in. Henry swallowed hard.

"Will you accept this mission?" asked the dragon in a stern-but-gentle tone, standing framed in the doorway.

Henry took a moment to answer the question. He drifted off, staring blankly into space. His eyes looked to be a million miles away. He found himself absorbing every detail of the dragon's appearance.

Suddenly, he caught a glimpse of himself in one of the scaly mirrors. There he was, reflected in it, frail and scrawny-looking. Henry was so close to it now that his nose was nearly touching that of his reflection. And slowly, Henry looked deep into his own hazel eyes and saw into an uncharted window. For the first time in his life, Henry was looking into his very soul. He blinked and then tore his eyes away. He had reached a decision.

Henry paused, gazed blearily at his bubbling concoction, which was now releasing a purplish mist, turned back, and nodded. *It can wait,* he thought sulkily.

"Splendid!" said the dragon, thrashing his head upward. "I must say, a noble choice. Climb aboard, Henry. We haven't much time."

Then something spectacular happened.

A crystal-blue web of light appeared overhead between a grouping of pine trees. It looked like a giant spider web that swayed with the sound of the wind. Every few seconds, it spit miniature lightening bolts.

This was definitely the most memorable moment of Henry's life. Deep inside, he somehow knew that this was going to be a profound experience—an experience soon to be much more than he'd expected.

Henry stepped confidently forward.

"My name is Zor," the dragon added, as Henry put his foot on the top of his wing and clambered onto his back. Henry wasn't sure where to hold on; everything in front of him was scaly and covered in spikes.

Henry was in a world of his own as he straddled the dragon's enormous back. He wondered. How many kids get to ride on the back of the Bahamut Dragon? Not many, he thought humbly.

More than ever, he wanted to help other kids. Maybe even give them hope during these trying times. He cast one last, excited-but-nervous look at the silent house and smiled. This was his chance to do something great.

Zor suddenly reared onto his hind legs, so that Henry had to grab his spiked neck to stay on.

At last, expansive wings billowed out on either side of Henry; he just had time to clutch Zor around the neck as best he could before they rose into the air.

"Hold on tight, Henry!" roared Zor as they rose upward. "We will project ourselves into the year 2010 when America is experiencing the worst recession since recorded history. Our first stop is Pennsylvania!"

The garage roof fell away, dropping out of sight as they lifted above the treetops. The clear, dark sky blossomed with stars and the moon cast an unreal light over the Fickle estate.

And together, they shot through the crystal-blue web and soared toward a different full moon.

CHAPTER FIVE

Henry stared at the back of Zor's head, which was dappled silver in the moonlight. A cool breeze whipped his hair and whistled in his ears. Although it was the year 2010, Henry couldn't tell the difference. Squinting through the darkness, the glistening lawns of the twenty-first century Windy Drive lay silent below him.

For one glorious minute, Henry was immersed in the sound of flapping wings. He couldn't believe it. He was actually flying. He wrapped his arms around Zor's neck, grinning from ear to ear.

"Whoa-a-a!" breathed Henry, looking back at the shrinking rooftops. "This is so cool. Wait 'til I tell Uncle Berk. He'll never believe it."

Henry was now a boy with a mission. He took in the inky sky with its twinkling stars and started to laugh; for a whole minute, he couldn't stop.

It was as though he was transported into a fantastic dream. This, thought Henry, was definitely the way to travel—high above a few lingering clouds with a cool breeze in his face, and the thought of seeing nosey Mr. Collingsworth's face when he flew past his house. A sudden idea struck him.

"Hold on!" said Henry in a loud whisper, a grin breaking across his face. "It's 2010—the grumpy, old neighbor would be deceased … yes, someone *new* would be living in his house." Henry took a deep sigh of relief.

The Bahamut Dragon had exceeded his expectations. He'd no idea communication with this glorious creature was possible. It was like magic!

Over time, it would become more and more evident that the Platinum Dragon was the king of all good dragons. After all, Zor was a team player in Henry's important mission.

In an unexpected burst of speed, Zor soared across the night sky.

"Sweet-t-t!" breathed Henry, holding on even tighter than before. The wind was pressing tight to his face as he glanced back. Willow Creek was now a blur. Only the glinting lights behind told him a town was miles away.

Henry was totally immersed in the moment. He never knew how much fun flying on a dragon could be, until now.

Hours later, Zor had covered a lot of landmass when Henry noticed they started descending. Just up ahead, Henry spotted an enormous lake.

"Lake Erie," said Zor suddenly, answering Henry's question.

"Cool-l-l!" shouted Henry, squinting through the darkness below.

Zor soared high above the dark waters, known as Lake Erie, the fourth largest lake of the five Great Lakes in North America. It was a spectacular sight. The moon danced across the sparkling waters like fairy dust.

Soon after, Zor made a sudden dip, as they reached the Gem City of Erie, Pennsylvania, the fourth largest city, after Philadelphia, Pittsburgh and Allentown. Then they flew over Presque Isle State Park.

Henry was glad he paid attention in history class. He was particularly fond of Pennsylvania, because it was known for its unique family attractions and historic sites.

Zor made an abrupt turn and headed southeast, passing over the old rooftops of Johnstown.

Just up ahead, they glided along the east bank of the Susquehanna River and over Harrisburg, the state capital. It was a stunning sight to see with its twinkling lights and quaint city streets.

The sky lightened very slowly, its inky blackness diluting to deepest blue. The landscape quickly turned wilder. The city life was gone and was replaced by tidy fields, woods, twisting streams and dark green hills.

The air was suddenly filled with the sweet smell of chocolate. Henry's mouth watered as he caught a glimpse of the street lamps that were shaped like Hershey's Kisses.

The famous town of Hershey with its many attractions, has become a popular destination for vacationing tourists. The imaginative entrepreneur, Milton S. Hershey had built Hershey Park in 1907. The sweet chocolate was once a luxury item for the wealthy, but now, it was affordable to all.

Henry's eyes had a habit of widening any time he passed by a chocolate shop. He craned around and tilted his head below. He so wished he could taste the scrumptious confections ...

But it was too late. They already passed *Hershey's Chocolate World*.

When he turned back, he thought he saw Zor wink, but when he looked again, the eyes were still as can be. Henry shook his head. The mysterious events continued to baffle him.

A minute later, as they flew past a large parking lot, a street cleaner rounded a corner.

For a split second, the man didn't realize what he had seen—then he jerked his head out the window to look up again and almost crashed into a street pole.

"AAAAH," he yelled, as he yanked the wheel just in time. With one eye glued to the road, the man quickly looked up through the wide window, as if looking for something.

Henry craned his head around. "Hello-o-o!" shouted Henry, waving his free hand gingerly as they soared overhead. "Nice evening, isn't it sir?"

The man was rattled. Almost at once, he brought the truck to a screeching halt and leapt out of the parked vehicle. He stared suspiciously into the clear sky, but saw nothing. The man gave his head a shake. What could he have been thinking of? It was early morning ... yes, that would be it. Come to think of it, he was feeling groggy and had trouble staying awake.

He hurried to his truck and set off down the road, feeling rather foolish. He cranked the gears and continued on, while mumbling words under his breath.

Zor descended lower. Henry saw a dark patchwork of fields and clumps of trees. They were skimming the treetops, a ray of moonlight illuminating the branches. The enormous wings, as wide as a small airplane, suddenly turned further southeast. Henry leaned in, like a passenger on a motorcycle, and adjusted his body with the shift in flight. The scenery was replaced by green fields that gave way in turn to acres of golden corn crops.

In the distance, the historic city of Philadelphia with its famous Liberty Bell was coming closer and closer, but before they arrived, Zor made an abrupt northeasterly turn. They followed a popular road called, Interstate 476, which is known as the Northeastern Extension, and continued onward.

Where was the secret headquarters?

A faint pinkish glow was now visible along the horizon.

Zor made another aerial turn over another well-traveled road called, Route 22 and headed east.

"We've made excellent time," announced Zor, tilting his head to peer at Henry. "We've got ten minutes."

"Huh?"

Zor suddenly reduced his speed and was now gliding gracefully across the sky. They tilted right and then exited over a street called, Airport Road.

Seconds later, Henry spotted something below.

Where were they?

Zor circled over the same massive complex. Although Zor hadn't mentioned where the secret headquarters was hidden in the huge state, somehow, Henry knew this was the place.

There was no sign of anyone moving about the area, not even a cleaning crew.

Then he saw it.

Towering 90-feet above ground level, a giant Coca-Cola bottle sat on top of the videoboard. The display read:

Coca-Cola Park

"—home of the Lehigh Valley IronPigs," said Zor at once.

"What?"

Henry burst out laughing, his expression changing from puzzlement to amusement. Then Henry's smirk was wiped clean, as they circled directly over the official ballpark.

"Whoa-a-a!" breathed Henry, squinting to get a closer look. His mind instantly recalled the thrill of eating a few hot dogs with an ice-cold, thirst-quenching, Coke bottle, while watching an exciting baseball game. Henry's mouth suddenly felt dry.

Coca-Cola Park is considered the Crown Jewel of Minor League Baseball. The ballpark continues to receive an unmatched level of excitement and fanfare in the Lehigh Valley and surrounding regions. It boasts a 360-degree concourse, allowing fans to enjoy family-fun amenities without missing a pitch. Supposedly, every time the IronPigs score a home run, the giant bottle comes to life, shooting bright fireworks into the sky.

Henry's mind raced as Zor, once again, circled over the huge field, as if contemplating a smooth landing. Henry's head exploded with questions. Is this the secret headquarters? Where was the room located? Where was the entryway? But more importantly, does anyone else know of its existence? His forehead wrinkled with effort, but nothing surfaced.

Henry's curiosity got the best of him. If it were true—if it's really the much-talked about headquarters, then why would it be located in the middle of a professional baseball field? It didn't make any logical sense. Unknown to Henry, the answers he'd been seeking were moments away.

Only a dull, orangeish tinge along the horizon showed that daybreak was drawing closer.

Henry settled back, thinking ... when are we going to land? He started to grow impatient, fidgeting and twisting on Zor's back. He had to know more. He tilted his head below for the tenth time. *What is Zor waiting for?*

At that moment, a glimpse of sunlight rose over the horizon, casting a sliver of light across the pitcher's mound.

"Three ..." roared Zor, one eye on Henry, "two ... one ..."

At last, Zor's head pointed toward the ground. Henry had to adjust to the change of position, just as Zor went into a nosedive, heading straight toward the pitcher's mound ...

"AAAAAAAAAAARAGH!"

They were almost there, and then, suddenly, they vanished.

CHAPTER SIX

It happened immediately: Henry felt a tug at his stomach. They were speeding downward in a deafening howl of wind and swirling color; the force of wind pulling them magnetically forward. He held on for dear life, trying to keep his eyes open, but the roller-coaster type feeling made him feel sick. They suddenly slowed—squinting he saw a blurred room beyond—his stomach churning—he closed his eyes again. And then, just as he had begun to worry about what would happen when they hit—

Zor's powerful feet slammed into solid ground, almost knocking Henry off his back. Henry looked around, feeling very windswept.

"At last, my boy!" cried Zor, as he bent his front knees and sank to the stone floor. "A marvelous trip!" There was a note of delight in his voice.

Henry slid clumsily off Zor's back and got gingerly to his feet. He was stiff from being hunched over for so many hours. He stretched his back, noticing that his legs seemed to be made of marshmallow.

He stood in a dimly lit chamber with a vaulted ceiling lost in darkness, tall enough to house the mighty dragon. The vacant room was still, as though it knew guests had arrived.

The secret headquarters was a wondrous place. It was cleverly hidden beneath Coca-Cola Park Baseball Stadium. Who would have guessed? And the entryway happened to be *through* the pitcher's mound!

Henry allowed himself a private laugh. *IronPigs?* The chosen name was rather amusing. What a funny title, he thought smugly. He immediately remembered the pickled pig snout—the ingredient in his secret invention. What an odd coincidence, he thought.

"I don't believe it," said Henry in a stunned voice, "this is awesome!"

Zor looked bemusedly at Henry, while furling and unfurling his wings.

Before Henry's wide eyes was a long, wooden table with velvet-red, high-back chairs. The room was lit by hundreds of glowing torches that hung on the stone walls. And in the middle of the room, was a circular area. A huge, thin plate of glass floated *in midair* over a giant globe of the earth.

Henry watched, fascinated, as three-dimensional images flashed across the translucent surface. His eyes gleamed with crazed enthusiasm, as different countries flashed across the glass.

Maybe it was scanning in sequence, Henry thought wildly, that seemed the logical thing—noticing that Zor was now staring at the flashing holographic images, he stared at it too. For a few seconds, there was complete silence. Then the picture changed. It zoomed in on a specific location.

Henry stood rooted to the spot. A sudden splash of color began to take form across the thin surface. A huge landmass came into focus. Henry immediately recognized the image as the United States of America.

Moments later, Henry grew bored and was ready for something different. He waited anxiously for the image to change, but the United States remained floating across the glass. *Why wasn't it changing?* he thought, his eyes wandering around the room. *Is this it?*

Almost at once, the image magnified, until Henry was staring at the state of Pennsylvania.

"Whoa-a-a!" breathed Henry, eyes fixed unblinkingly at the spectacular sight. He stepped forward to get a closer view.

Instantly, the panoramic scene zoomed in on eastern Pennsylvania.

Henry's eyebrows raised as nine counties called Lehigh, Carbon,

Berks, Northampton, Monroe, Bucks, Montgomery, Chester and Delaware magnified across the glass.

Henry figured they were the ones they'd visit first. Then the other counties would follow.

"Um—Zor?"

"Yes, Henry?" said Zor, who was now standing beside him.

"Are these—"

"Yes," said Zor placidly, anticipating his question.

Henry drifted off. What would the kids think when he showed up at their school riding a dragon? What would the teachers think? But most importantly, what would he say to lift their spirits? Henry's mind was spinning over the same unanswerable questions.

A slight breeze lifted Henry's hair. He sensed a presence. His heart raced, as he quickly spun around.

Shortly after, a cool shiver traveled up and down his spine.

Before Henry had time to think, a whirlwind traveled across the room ...

Walking across the stone floor, as if in slow motion, was an old woman.

CHAPTER SEVEN

For maybe a minute—a glorious minute, Henry stared for what seemed like an eternity. He had never seen a woman quite like this one. Her striking features left Henry mesmerized. A sudden burst of flame from the torches revealed her intense eyes, which were so penetrating, that Henry had trouble looking at her directly.

Her body was short, plump and old. Her black hair was streaked with white like a skunk. She wore a shabby green dress that was tied with a purple sash. And around her neck, dangled all sorts of stones and crystals.

"I see you've arrived on schedule," screeched the old woman, holding a carved walking stick. "Delighted you could make it."

Henry was intrigued. How did she get here? Come to think of it, he didn't hear anyone enter the room—

"Please join me, Henry," said the woman, who was pouring boiling water over a sweet-smelling tea bag. "I'm very partial to herbal teas. Did you enjoy your trip?"

Henry nodded and then said, "H-How did you know my name? I don't believe we've met."

The woman's face formed into a smile, which looked quite pleasant to see. With an eyebrow half raised and a gleam in her eye, she gently brushed her streaked hair from her face.

"Well, Mr. Fickle, I've known your name since you were born—let's just say, I expected your arrival." Her eyes lingered on him.

Henry looked surprised by her bold words.

"Huh?"

"My name is Lady Norton," the woman added, as she flopped herself down on a plush chair.

After a nervous glance at Zor, who nodded encouragingly, Henry stepped forward.

Lady Norton abruptly turned toward Zor. "Oh, pleased to see you again, my dear friend." Then she turned back to Henry.

The Platinum Dragon bowed in silence.

Henry's eyes widened. Did they know each other?

Moments later, Zor walked quietly across the room, as if to give them privacy.

Henry scanned the woman with intense curiosity. The woman, although clearly old, radiated such an abundance of vitality that Henry felt hypnotized by what was sitting before him.

For a minute, neither of them spoke.

Henry felt happy to be invited to the secret headquarters, standing far below the ground, underneath a well-known baseball field. Who would believe it? Certainly not anyone in Willow Creek, he thought bitterly, shaking his head. After an uncomfortable silence, Henry spoke.

"Er—it's a pleasure to meet you," he mumbled politely. "M-May I ask a question?"

Lady Norton gave a wide smile and nodded.

"Who are you?" he asked in a curious tone. "I mean," Henry went on, "why have you been expecting *me?*" He sank into a comfortable chair across from Lady Norton, who was sipping tea.

Lady Norton peered over her cup, giving Henry a searching stare. Her tense gaze made Henry feel as though he were being X-rayed.

"Well, that's an interesting question," said Lady Norton, smiling pleasantly, "and quite a long story—but if you don't mind, we must leave it for another time."

Henry nodded.

Lady Norton surveyed Henry, her eyes twinkling. "When the student is ready, the teacher appears," she said in a gentle tone. "Think of me as your teacher, Henry."

Henry's eyebrows raised. The only teachers he knew taught at

Willow Creek Elementary. He sat, thinking … no, Lady Norton was definitely different. Nothing like this woman had ever been seen in Willow Creek.

Lady Norton just smiled knowingly. "No need to concern yourself," she said at once. "We won't be working together for a while—well, until your *mission* is complete." She reached for her piping-hot cup and took another sip of tea.

Mission?

At this last word, the room was filled with a silence so absolute that Henry lost his breath.

After what seemed a long while, Lady Norton spoke.

"Ah—I have something to discuss with you, Henry. It's about your … *mission*." Her eyes twinkled in the flickering light.

"What?"

Henry was surprised. How did Lady Norton know about his secret task? He couldn't imagine where she'd gotten the information, unless she learned it from Zor. But that was impossible, he thought. He only decided to accept Zor's proposal earlier that morning.

Lady Norton chuckled, as if she knew what Henry was thinking. "No need to concern yourself," she said cheerfully. "I'm here to help."

Henry opened his mouth, but Lady Norton was busy pouring them both another cup of tea from a dainty-looking pot.

Then something startling happened.

As Henry stared dreamily into space, an image flashed in his head. Henry's heart raced. Somehow, he *knew* what to say to the kids, but it seemed too simple. He started to dismiss the idea, thinking … yes, it was way too easy. He must have been mistaken. Then Lady Norton interrupted his thoughts.

"Your *mission*, as one might say, is your true calling," said Lady Norton, looking directly into Henry's hazel eyes. Then her eyes narrowed. "Things don't always have to be complicated, dear. Humans have a funny habit of making things difficult, you see. Never underestimate your visions, Henry, they will always reveal the truth."

Henry nodded in agreement, feeling rather foolish.

At that moment, Henry decided to never doubt himself again.

It may have been only seconds, but to Henry the moment was life-changing. Instantly, he felt a connection with this woman whom he'd met only moments ago. Finally, someone understood him.

CHAPTER EIGHT

It was agreed Henry would travel with Zor to the nine counties in Pennsylvania that he'd seen earlier. His intuition had been correct. Afterwards, they'd return to the secret headquarters to find out the next group of counties, and so on, and so forth, until they had visited the entire state. Then they would receive further instructions.

The vivid vision that flashed in his mind only moments ago, had also been correct. It was all very strange. The entire scene, which occurred in an instant, explained everything in complete detail. It felt as though a program had been downloaded into his brain. He knew exactly what to do.

Henry clearly saw himself handing out collectable cards … the Bahamut Dragon printed across its glossy surface … for every kid … in every elementary school across America.

The unique card would represent one task they had to accomplish. Zor and Henry would challenge them to give back to their community by helping a family member, friend or neighbor. Some examples would include, mowing an older neighbors grass, shoveling snow from their driveway, planting flowers, organizing a food drive, or baking a batch of cookies for someone who was feeling sad. The ideas were unlimited and so were the results.

Henry drew a great shuttering breath, as the bigger picture flashed in his head. He sat, thinking … yes, it's during these difficult times that communities would pull together. As if by magic, people would feel lighter, making their temporary troubles fade away—but one haunting question remained. Where would he get the millions of collectable cards? Lady Norton's screechy voice jolted him back to the room.

"I'm proud of you, Henry," said Lady Norton, patting him gently on the shoulder. "You have no idea the impact you will make in America by this simple-but-powerful act of kindness. Children everywhere will remember your name. Because of your good deed, they will blossom into fine citizens."

Henry felt the heat rush to his face.

"Er ... thanks," Henry muttered, not sure how to respond. "I think—"

Henry never got a chance to finish, when Lady Norton spoke a few words.

"I see you're coming along well with your projects."

A look of great excitement suddenly dawned on Henry's face. He didn't have the slightest idea how she knew such personal things, but it didn't matter. He was beginning to feel more comfortable with her. He humbly nodded.

Lady Norton smiled and then continued. "I see you have added pig snout to the mixture—*brilliant!*"

The chamber rang with laughter. After all, who would think of such a thing?

Henry sensed he might not get a chance to visit with the wise woman again—well, anytime soon. It was his grand opportunity to pour out his short life's experiences.

Lady Norton listened. Her dark eyes were glimmering in the flickering light. Zor's mouth crinkled in a funny kind of way, as if pleased with Henry's addictive enthusiasm.

Henry spoke of his earlier childhood and the difficulties he had struggled with, how others shunned his special abilities. He spoke of his parents, how his dear mother died, and of the day his father and mean stepmother moved them to Willow Creek. He mentioned he met a few friends, but they never lasted too long. He explained that Uncle Berk was his true friend. He delved deep into his experiments in the garage. He took pride in telling her about the cool things he invented. He told her of his most cleverest invention yet, and how he was very close at arriving at a bright solution. He was convinced he was missing a few more ingredients.

He concluded with a few lingering thoughts on how happy he was to have met her, and how Zor, during their journey there, taught him to believe in himself. Although he's just a kid, his *mission* wasn't impossible to achieve—well, unless he *thought* it was.

Lady Norton yawned. "Oh, dear," she said abruptly, looking distressed. She stood up at once. "It's nine in the morning and I'm late for a meeting." She slurped the last sip of tea and placed the cup on a nearby table. "And you have a task to attend to."

"Oh, Miss Norton," whined Henry, staring around the room, "must you leave so soon?"

"I'm afraid so," said Lady Norton, getting herself together. "Now remember your assigned destinations."

"Yes, but ..." said Henry grimly, "it's just ..."

"Your *mission*—yes, you'll know what to do when the time comes, dear. Zor will take you to each elementary school in Pennsylvania." She turned suddenly. "Oh, it's quite a challenge, dear, but the rewards—well, are much greater than yourself." Her eyes widened.

Henry nodded and then turned to look at Zor, who was now standing a few feet away. His heart sank. He wished he'd more *time*. He quickly turned and said, "When will I see—"

But Lady Norton was gone. Instead, Henry was staring at an unoccupied space. She departed so suddenly and silently you'd think she sank below the ground.

Lady Norton's distinct voice spoke suddenly in the room. It seemed to reverberate through the air, bouncing off the walls.

Henry quickly spun around, but Lady Norton was nowhere in sight.

"Oh, a tidbit of information. Better listen carefully, dear. Unicorn Hair is very ancient, you see. I must say, I find the ingredient very magical. Yes, well, ponder over it ..."

Lady Norton's screechy voice traveled upward toward the cavern ceiling and faded from the room.

"Unicorn Hair?" Henry said blankly, wondering why he didn't think of it.

Henry drifted off. Could it be that he was one ingredient away from finding a solution? And, if the wise woman was correct, she would become the coolest teacher he ever met.

"What's *that?*" Henry asked Zor, looking up at the vaulted ceiling.

But the dragon remained oddly silent.

Henry watched something fall gracefully downwards, as though it carried the weight of a leaf. It slowly made its way to the stone floor. When it was only inches from his head, Henry reached up and snatched it.

And then he saw it.

Henry couldn't speak; a grin slowly formed over his face. It got wider and wider.

Before Henry's bulging, hazel-colored eyes, was a collectable card—the same one from his vision. He stood speechless, as he stared into the catlike eyes of the Bahamut Dragon.

"Better move aside, Henry," said Zor in a calm-but-firm tone.

"Huh?"

Another card came whizzing down from the darkened ceiling as he went to speak and pelted his head.

"Ouch!"

Next moment, thousands and thousands of cards came shooting from above like bullets. Henry leapt for cover just in time.

From a safe distance, Henry and Zor watched the cards still piling into the room, bouncing off the floor. Henry gaped, open-eyed at Zor, who was nodding knowingly.

When the rain shower of cards subsided, an invisible team started sweeping small piles into manageable sacks. It was all very strange, as though the room was tidying up and preparing them for their trip.

In a rush of joy, Henry Fickle realized he'd received one last gift from Lady Norton.

CHAPTER NINE

Now, with the sun newly risen, and a large sack of cards straddling Zor's back, it was time to press on. It was only just dawning on Henry how many elementary schools there must be in the entire state of Pennsylvania.

Henry sighed very deeply, as he scrambled clumsily onto Zor's back, gripping tightly around his neck.

An extraordinary lightness seemed to spread through his whole body and the next second, in a rush of enormous flapping wings, they were flying upward toward the cavern ceiling. They rocketed upward so steeply that Henry had to clench his arms and legs tightly around Zor to avoid sliding backward. He closed his eyes and put his face down into the dragon's scaly skin.

The air was whipping through Henry's hair. And before he knew it, they both disappeared through the pitcher's mound and soared out into a sun-filled sky.

Henry could not believe how fast they moved: Zor soared over the memorable home of the Lehigh Valley IronPigs, his wings hardly beating. The warm air was brushing Henry's face; eyes blurred against the rushing wind. He cast one last, excited look at Coca-Cola Park with its giant ballpark and smiled.

A new feeling overtook Henry's heart—a feeling that he never felt before. This, thought Henry, was surely the only way to travel—past fluffy clouds, on the back of a mighty dragon, bright sunlight in his face with no care in the world, and the prospect of seeing teachers faces when they landed smoothly on sweeping lawns of schools everywhere. For the first time, Henry smiled from the inside.

For some reason, Zor decided to take a scenic tour over historic Bethlehem, passing rows of quaint stores, including Moravian

Book Shop.

Henry's heart gave a jolt. He loved bookstores. Since he was eight, he must have read hundreds of books, including the works of great inventors.

In the brilliant sunlight, Henry spotted rows of rooftops. Zor made an abrupt turn and headed east over Route 22 on which a heavy volume of cars were speeding toward their destinations. Suddenly, Henry witnessed an unusual sequence of fender-benders.

"Um—I think they saw us," muttered Henry, glancing below.

"I do believe you're right, Henry," said Zor automatically, as if unconcerned about being seen.

Henry had no idea what school they'd visit first, but it didn't matter. He was enjoying the ride, acting like an interested tourist.

As they covered the entire state of Pennsylvania, they must have passed hundreds of landmarks that were filled with historic tales. His eyes would widen every time they glided over popular destinations like Hawk Mountain Sanctuary, Ringing Rocks Park, Crystal Cave, Bushkill Falls, the Philadelphia Zoo, and Dorney Park & Wild Water Kingdom with its breath-taking rides and attractions. And across from the huge park, was the scrumptious Ice Cream World!

Henry's mouth watered. He wished he could taste their wide-selection of homemade flavors. He was particularly fond of berry ice cream, over-flowing with gobs of hot fudge and crumbled sweet candies. Henry sat grumbling when Zor had to remind him of his important mission.

Henry sighed deeply.

At that moment, the Bahamut Dragon became his friend. There are some adventures you can't share without ending up liking each other, and inspiring thousands of kids across Pennsylvania was one of them.

CHAPTER TEN

It all happened so quickly, as if time stood still. Henry had lost all sense of how far they had traveled; all his faith was in the dragon below him; still streaking purposefully through the sky, barely flapping his wings as he sped ever onward.

* ❂✳⟩ *

Earlier that morning, while landing across the velvety-green lawn of their very first school, Henry received a startling surprise.

Henry stood in the grass, straining with the hefty sack of cards slumped over his shoulder, when the clever dragon suddenly transformed into an old man, accompanied by seven golden canaries.

"Well, you don't want to give folks a scare, do you?" screeched the old man, ambling slowly toward the front doors, the canaries circling above his head.

Henry frowned. He desperately wanted other kids to see him arriving on the back of a dragon.

Now, he'd have to speak to students and faculty members, while standing next to an old man and seven fluttering canaries. Henry rolled his eyes at the bright sky. If the birds weren't odd-looking enough, he thought, his face reddening.

But for some strange reason, the canaries were a hit among teachers and students. They found them to be very entertaining. Their faces glowed with enthusiasm, and their longing eyes revealed their simmering questions. Students would gather around the old gentleman, asking all sorts of questions and begging for his training methods. The old man was more than happy to tell his magical tale in great detail.

"… they like when you sing to them," he told them, as he whistled a happy tune.

"Ohhhh," groups of girls would say together, watching the unusually friendly canaries flutter around the room.

Meanwhile, the boys were more interested in the collectable cards.

"Totally awesome," they would say in an excited tone. "Check out his catlike eyes …"

Everyone was talking at once. And eventually, Henry couldn't help but laugh. After all, the old man was rather amusing.

So after visiting every elementary school in America, it was one of those rare moments when the expanded story was even more interesting than the original one. Everyone listened with great interest, while Henry shook his head. Thanks to his wise old friend, the story of the seven golden canaries got better each time.

* ⊙✳ ⁾ *

Before Henry knew it, his mission was complete. Exhausted, stomach rumbling, mind spinning over the dramatic events of the long trip, Henry was anxious to return home. *Wherever that was,* Henry thought tiredly.

But during their flight toward Willow Creek, unknown to Henry, a magical thing was happening across twenty-first century America. News reporters from every media outlet across the nation were reporting a miraculous shift in the economy. Things were not only improving, but acts of kindness were spreading like wildfire through every neighborhood and every school corridor. Then the hottest news hit the Internet.

Within moments, a stream of hungry Bloggers recorded their personal thoughts across social networking sites, including Facebook, Twitter and MySpace. Apparently, the hottest incident had reached the evening news:

"And finally, sky-watchers everywhere have reported a strange object in the sky. There have been millions of sightings of a—well, a dragon soaring in every direction since sunrise. Experts are unable to explain it and are convinced it was some sort of prank." The newscaster allowed himself a chuckle. "Most unusual. And now, over to the weather—"

* ⊙✳ ⁾ *

At last, standing outside the garage, back in the early 1930s, Henry cast one last, admirable look at the Bahamut Dragon and bowed his head slightly. He'd trouble finding the right words to describe his gratitude. So instead, he mentally thanked the noble creature in silence.

A second later, as though Zor read his mind, winked in his direction. Maybe he was imagining it; maybe not. The dragon turned his mighty frame around, peered over his back and said, "I do believe you have an invention to attend to, Henry."

"Yeah," muttered Henry, staring blankly into space. "I suppose so." His mind was already searching where to find the Unicorn Hair. "Er … thanks," muttered Henry sluggishly, his eyes starting to feel heavy.

Zor bent his head slightly. "Yes, well, until we meet again …"

The Platinum Dragon gave a mighty roar and lifted into the night air. When Henry looked again, silhouetted against the full moon, and growing smaller by the moment, was the king of all good dragons. His expansive wings were now miles away, flapping gracefully across the starry sky. For some strange reason, the stars seemed to blink uncontrollably, as if honoring his presence.

Henry gazed after Zor … then a cloud drifted across the moon …
Zor was gone.

Henry turned, knowing they'd meet again. Then the room faded.
Henry Fickle slipped into nothingness.

CHAPTER ELEVEN

Something blurry was hovering above him. Zor! He tried reaching out, but his arms were weak.

He blinked. It wasn't Zor. It was someone else.

He blinked again. The concerned face of Uncle Berk focused into view.

"Wake-up, Henry!" shouted Uncle Berk, shaking him. "I made breakfast. You don't want to be late for school, do you? Were you working late, again?" Uncle Berk grinned, turned, and walked briskly out of the garage.

"Huh?"

Henry woke with a start. He found himself slumped over the workbench. He straightened up and squinted around the silent room. What happened? He stared around in disbelief, as his heart sank horribly. *Was it all a dream?*

He tried to remember the dream he'd been having. It was really strange. He was on the back of the Bahamut Dragon, flying toward Pennsylvania. It seemed so real. Zor, the magic dragon, was talking to him about his important *mission* … he spoke of all the children he'd inspire … they would arrive at the secret headquarters … he met Lady Norton … they were flying across Pennsylvania … then America …

Suddenly, Henry felt wide-awake.

School!

Henry sprang up. Panic flooded through him. If he were late— if he missed another class—well, he'd be spending the *entire* afternoon in detention. Henry couldn't bare the terrible thought. He bolted toward the wide doors.

Something caught Henry's attention.

Lying on the dirt floor was a collectable card.

"What the—"

He bent down and snatched the familiar card in his hands. He held it close to his face and saw, to his great surprise, Bahamut, the Platinum Dragon with his stark blue eyes.

Henry's eye's bulged.

"No way!" he whispered to himself.

Henry stared at the rare card. The vertical pupils shifted suddenly. He drew his face back when one of the catlike eyes winked.

"What the—"

The card magically transformed before his wide eyes. Squinting slightly, Henry saw a wrinkly face … then a slight smile … then a head of gray hair form over the distinct face of the dragon.

"Whoa-a-a," breathed Henry, as he stood in awe.

The picture seemed to take its time developing.

Henry stared—and the wise face of an old man with seven yellow canaries stared back.

Henry laughed privately to himself.

"Hold on!" he said suddenly.

The memory of what happened hit him. I *was* flying with Zor! He ran outside and craned his neck around. Although the dragon wasn't there, the fancy card was enough to prove it had really happened.

Henry's mind raced. Should he tell Uncle Berk or the few friends he had at school? Something held him back. It would be a difficult story to believe. He slid the card into his back pocket, not wanting to diminish the magic. For the first time, Henry decided to keep a secret to himself.

At that moment, Henry felt different. He had accomplished something very important. Others would have considered it an impossible feat, but Henry wasn't like everyone else. His mind didn't work that way.

Over time, the memory had faded. Although Henry was hungrily working on his latest invention, America would never forget his selfless deed. Lady Norton had been correct. Henry Fickle's name was remembered.

At this very moment, unknown to the young inventor, Zor and Lady Norton were meeting in secret and were saying in excited voices, "To Henry Fickle—the boy who will change the world!"

To learn about our children's publishing company called,
The Sorcerer's Press and read more note-worthy books by this
author like the popular, hardcover, *Henry Fickle Trilogy*, visit:
www.henryfickle.net

Look for book one, *Henry Fickle and the Secret Laboratory*,
which was nominated a finalist in *ForeWord Magazines*
juvenile Book-of-the-Year awards!
And book two, *Henry Fickle and the Time Capsule*,
both available from The Sorcerer's Press.

The author lives in Pennsylvania and is currently
working on the much-anticipated, last installment
in the *Henry Fickle Trilogy*, as well as a 10-book
paperback series that will have fans
thirsting for more!

ATTENTION ALL FICKLE FANS!

If you'd like to join our Mailing List to find out
when the NEXT *Henry Fickle* book arrives hot
off the press, please send us your
Name, Full Mailing Address and Email to:

The Sorcerer's Press
P.O. Box 710
Trexlertown, PA 18087

Questions? Call The Sorcerer's Press at 484-241-5424.
Or sent us an email: sorcererspress@aol.com
If you'd like to order
Henry Fickle and the Magic Dragon of Pennsylvania
for friends or family, please send a check for $6.95,
plus $3.00 shipping for one book and $2.00 for
each additional book to the address above.
Please include the person(s) name for autographing!

HENRY FICKLE'S
MAGICAL CHALLENGE

Henry Fickle, the eccentric inventor, and Zor, the Bahamut Dragon, has assigned a task, which will test your skills and your character. Will you accept the challenge? *Yes?* We're delighted! Well, then, shall we get started? Let the challenge begin!

First, cut out the collectable card on the next page (you or your parents can laminate it!). This, my dear friends, will be *your* dragon card. It will remind you of your noble deed.

Next, choose a family member, friend or neighbor. Then think of a "good deed," without expecting anything in return, and do something nice for that person. If you are eager to help more than one person, we commend you for your efforts. When your task is complete, you'll be part of our loyal team. Together, we'll create a new America by our selfless deeds, which will return to us many fold!

BAHAMUT DRAGON

Existing since the beginning of time, Bahamut, the Platinum Dragon, is ever watchful for the cause of lawful good. He sits unsleeping in his palace on Mount Celestia, the Seven Heavens. He has limitless compassion for the weak, downtrodden and the helpless. He forgives easily, yet has no tolerance for evil in any form.

He is noble, wise, judicious, kind and helpful, but he can also be stern. By dragon standards, he's selfless and sharing, being neither vain nor desirous of treasure. He's highly respected and values wisdom, knowledge and song. He amplifies anything that's good and will offer protection to those who seek it. And when he wishes to interact with mortals, he appears as an old man, accompanied by seven golden canaries. He teaches his followers to always uphold the highest ideals of honor and justice, to be constantly vigilant against evil and to oppose it from all fronts, and to protect the weak, liberate the oppressed and defend just order!

BAHAMUT DRAGON

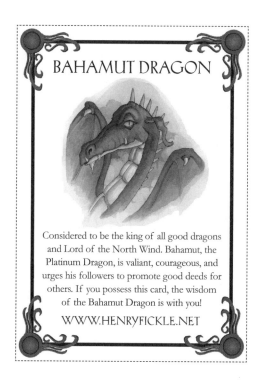

Considered to be the king of all good dragons and Lord of the North Wind. Bahamut, the Platinum Dragon, is valiant, courageous, and urges his followers to promote good deeds for others. If you possess this card, the wisdom of the Bahamut Dragon is with you!

WWW.HENRYFICKLE.NET